NOTHING
EVER
HAPPENS
HERE

NOTHING EVER HAPPENS HERE

BILL GILLHAM

Illustrated by LASZLO ACS

ANDRE DEUTSCH

First published in 1990
André Deutsch Limited
105 – 106 Great Russell Street, London WClB 3LJ

ISBN 0 233 98564 6

Typeset by AKM Associates (UK) Ltd
Ajmal House, Hayes Road, Southall

Printed and bound in Great Britain by
WBC, Bridgend, Mid Glam.

ONE

Joey Medallo looked out of the window of the Boeing 747 as it came into Heathrow Airport: if this was England he didn't think much of it.

The flight across the Atlantic had been boring, and the vacation looked like being boring as well.

He glanced at his mother who sat next to him. She was always nervous at take-off and landing but tried not to show it.

Joey's father was on the other side of her. Dr Medallo didn't look like a research physicist and a key figure in the SDI 'Star Wars' program. With his black curly hair and tall, athletic figure he looked more like a professional tennis player.

At ten years old Joey was recognisably a junior version of his father.

With a thud the wheels of the Boeing bumped down onto the runway and the engines went into reverse with a roaring, rushing sound.

As the plane slowed down it seemed to settle back more securely on the ground and Mrs Medallo relaxed.

'I can do without that kind of excitement,' she said, 'I know the pilot's done it thousands of times, but I always think: this time he's going to get it wrong.'

Joey pulled a face. 'I bet nothing exciting ever happens here. It looks kind of boring to me.'

Afterwards, they were to remember his words.

'Sure you've got all your hand luggage?'

Joey grinned: he knew why his father said that. His mother was always losing things but she got mad if you even suggested it.

People were leaving their seats now. Dr Medallo waited for another couple to go ahead of them down the aisle to the exit. Joey noticed that the man looked rather like his father, and the woman with him was blonde like his mother; even the same kind of hair style.

'You go ahead,' said the man, 'I'm afraid I walk very slowly.'

Dr Medallo nodded. 'I'm grateful,' he said, smiling; but the man made no reply, just waited until Joey and his parents had moved out from their seats.

'I guess he must have something wrong with his legs,' said Dr Medallo as they walked up the corridor from the entry gate.

His wife glanced back over her shoulder. 'He waves his hair,' she said, 'I don't trust men who have their hair waved.'

Joey looked at her curiously. 'How do you know that, mom?'

Mrs Medallo smoothed her own blonde hair.

'Women just know that sort of thing,' she said.

By the time they got to passport control the other couple were not even in sight.

'Do you expect anyone to meet us?' asked Mrs Medallo.

'No,' said her husband, 'the idea is that we go straight to the apartment that they've rented for us. The British Security Service will get in touch with us there. We just act like tourists.'

But the immigration officer who saw them at passport control must have known something because, having looked through their passports, he kept them for a few minutes while he made a telephone call.

'Sorry to hold you up,' he said with a smile; but he didn't explain.

As they turned the corner away from the passport section, a man wearing a dark blue raincoat stepped forward.

'Dr and Mrs Medallo?' he asked. 'My name is Conroy: Special Branch.'

And he produced a small official-looking card bearing his photograph. Dr Medallo glanced at it briefly and shrugged his shoulders.

'What's it all about?'

'We don't want you to go through the main concourse, for security reasons.'

Joey stared at the man. He had dark hair, cut very short, and the sort of expression that gave nothing away. He looked like a secret service man.

'I don't think we should waste any time.'

Dr Medallo hesitated. 'What about our luggage?'

'That'll be taken care of.'

'O.K.,' said Joey's father, 'I guess you know your own job.'

'This way.'

The man led them to a door marked 'Staff: Private'. He

took a key from his pocket and unlocked the door, glancing
to left and right as he did so.

What happened next all took place very quickly.

Joey went into the room first, followed by his parents.
Conroy came in last, relocking the door. Joey hardly noticed
that. He was too busy looking at the two men facing them
from the other side of a large table. One, a short, stocky man

of middle age, was seated. The other, tall and blond, with a tense watchful face, was standing. And in his hand he held a gun.

TWO

Before they could say anything Conroy had pushed Joey forward and the tall, blond man took him by the shoulder and pressed the gun against the side of his head. Joey could feel the muzzle, hard and cold, just above his ear.

'What the hell's going on?' Dr Medallo took a step forward, but his wife stopped him.

'Don't move! Joey, keep still!' Her voice was steady but Joey could see that her hands were shaking. 'We can see what's going on: they have to explain things to us.'

Joey looked at his mother without moving his head. He tried to smile but somehow he couldn't get his face to do it. The man's grip on his shoulder hurt him, but he wasn't going to show it: he pressed his lips together.

The man seated at the table smiled. Not exactly a friendly smile, but goodnatured; you could imagine him telling jokes in a bar and laughing at them himself. But his voice had a note of authority. 'If you just do as we ask, quickly and without argument, nobody will get hurt.'

The blond man gestured with his gun. 'Empty your pockets onto the table and put your hand luggage there as well; your handbag, if you please, Mrs Medallo.'

Mrs Medallo glanced at her husband. 'Don't argue, Mario, do as they say.'

The man seated at the table nodded approval. Even if he had said nothing you would have known that he was in charge.

The blond man saw Joey's father hesitate as he put his hand in his inside pocket.

'Everything,' he said.

Dr Medallo threw a couple of sealed envelopes onto the table. His face was dark with anger.

Conroy moved cautiously to the side of them, never taking his eyes off Joey's father, and swept everything except the briefcase into a large plastic carrier bag.

The man at the table spread his hands apologetically. 'I'm sorry I cannot offer you a chair,' he said, 'but impulsive people have been known to use chairs as weapons, and we shall not be here long.'

'Just who are you?' asked Joey's mother.

'My name is Andersen,' the man replied, 'and this little drama is very necessary to our plans. If you do exactly as we say there will be no problem. You and your husband will be kept together. Joey will be somewhere else. If you behave yourself, Joey will be quite safe. And you, Joey,' Andersen turned deliberately to face him, 'you can keep your parents safe by doing as you are told.' He held Joey's gaze for a moment to emphasise his words.

'What's it all about?' Dr Medallo had recovered his temper but there was something threatening in his tone. Joey saw Conroy slip his hand into his raincoat: he must have a gun too.

Andersen held up his hand, like a teacher explaining a

point in class. 'Simple,' he said, 'the brilliant and top secret Dr Medallo has come here to spend a month in a British research establishment working on part of the Star Wars program – which interests us very much. We plan to put two of our own people in place of yourself and your wife. To do that properly we need you out of the way, we need your papers. And we need Joey.'

There was silence. Andersen sat at the table, drumming his fingers lightly, and watching Joey's parents.

It was Mrs Medallo who spoke: her voice wasn't quite steady. 'Why do you need Joey?'

Andersen leant back in his chair.

'The people here are expecting Dr and Mrs Medallo and their son, Joey. I have a large number of people to choose from to replace you and your husband, including well-qualified physicists. A little cosmetic change, a detailed briefing, your documents and papers – and they are convincing. But unfortunately among my agents I don't have any ten year old boys who could pass as American. So I need the real thing.' He leant forward. 'All Joey has to do is to be himself.'

The man who called himself Conroy looked at his watch. 'It's time we were going.'

Andersen got to his feet. 'Come, Joey,' your "adoptive" parents are waiting. Our top secret Mr Conroy of British Intelligence will escort you to them.'

The man in the blue raincoat laughed. 'So secret they don't even know they've got me.'

Andersen ignored him. 'Kiss your mother goodbye, Joey.'

The blond man relaxed his grip on Joey's shoulder but still kept the gun pointed in his direction.

Mrs Medallo hugged him very tightly without speaking; his father put his hand under his chin. 'Joey,' he said, 'remember you're all we've got. So no heroics, just keep safe until we're back together again.'

Joey nodded. And the next moment he was hustled through the door on the other side of the room with the man called Conroy holding him firmly by the arm.

They walked quickly down a white-painted corridor, through a swing door and along another corridor with offices on one side. Joey could hear the hum of a computer print-out and then a telephone bleeping. There were people at work in the offices – but they all seemed busy and nobody paid them any attention. Through some double doors that opened automatically as they approached, and then they were onto the crowded concourse.

Conroy moved quickly forward: he obviously knew exactly where he was going. For the first time Joey noticed that he was carrying his father's briefcase and the carrier bag.

It was Joey who saw the couple from the plane first. From a distance they did look very much like his parents: and to someone who didn't know them . . .

Conroy had seen them: he tightened his grip on Joey's arm and as they moved in their direction, the woman got to her feet.

'Why, Joey!' she exclaimed. 'We thought you'd got lost.'

And at that precise moment Joey stopped being scared and started to be angry.

Close to, this woman didn't look a bit like his mother and here she was acting the part. And to people watching, it might look like the real thing: Joey resented that.

The woman took him by the hand and pulled him down to sit next to her. The two men were standing in close conversation. Conroy called the other man 'Paul': he was certainly remarkably like his father but thinner, his eyes not so blue and kind of distant. Paul addressed Conroy as 'Karl': probably his name wasn't Conroy at all. *Karl Conroy*: it didn't sound right.

'Chocolate, Joey?' The woman took a Hershey Bar from the

bag at her feet. Joey shook his head impatiently: he was watching the two men.

Karl seemed to be giving instructions. He handed over passports, keys, a wallet and the sealed envelopes from the carrier bag. Paul said very little but listened carefully. Still talking, Karl passed Mrs Medallo's handbag to the woman.

'That's my mother's,' said Joey.

'Sure it is,' said the woman, 'and I'm your pretend mother for now. Haven't you ever played pretend games, Joey?'

She treated him as though he was a kid.

Paul sat down and Karl turned to the woman. He started speaking in English but then, with a glance at Joey, lapsed into a language that Joey had never heard before. But if he couldn't understand the words Joey nonetheless realised that the man's tone was different. To Paul he had given instructions; with this woman he discussed things as an equal.

'Right,' said Karl, dropping back into English, 'what you do is take the subway, what they call the underground here. You need to get moving now, we don't want any hitches.'

He turned and walked back the way he had come. In a few moments he was swallowed up in the crowd.

The woman took Joey's hand in a surprisingly strong grip: he couldn't have got away. All the time she kept talking to him, smiling brightly. To any passer-by they would seem like mother and son.

The man who looked so much like his father walked beside them. Joey had the feeling he was a bit jumpy: the woman kept glancing at him.

They went down the steps to the underground. Paul bought the tickets: he seemed to have some difficulty explaining where he wanted to go.

The woman went through the automatic ticket barrier first, then Joey. Paul came last.

And even as the spokes of the barrier clicked round, Joey had an idea.

'No heroics,' his father had said: but if he judged it right heroics wouldn't come into it. What he had to do was to give these two no cause for concern until the moment came.

There was a train waiting at the platform. At first there were only a few people in it, but gradually it filled up.

Joey had been careful to take a seat almost opposite one of the doors. Paul sat facing him, the woman next to him. When she offered him a stick of gum he took it.

'Thanks,' he said, but without looking at her. He didn't want to appear too friendly.

'I think Joey and I are going to get along just fine,' said the woman.

Paul scowled at her. 'Sure,' he said, 'it's going to be one big happy family.'

The doors of the train started to close, catching Joey unawares. He'd missed his chance.

But they opened again, almost immediately starting to close for a second time.

Joey hurled himself forward, the edge of the doors brushing against his shoulders as he went through, rolling over and over on the platform.

As he sat up he saw the train moving out, carrying his 'pretend' parents with it.

THREE

As the train vanished down the tunnel, everything was suddenly still, the platform deserted except for a man approaching from the other end.

Joey got to his feet. A man in a blue raincoat: who had called himself 'Conroy' but whose real name was Karl.

Karl didn't hurry. He didn't need to. The only way out was behind him.

Joey was surprised how cool he felt. In only a few seconds Karl would be up to him, but he was thinking so fast that it seemed like a long time.

He walked towards him, as if to give himself up. There was still nobody else on the platform and their footsteps echoed. Quite close now.

'That was a stupid thing to do, Joey.'

Joey swung his arms, whistling, and then ran forward as if to get past on the side nearest the wall. Not for nothing was he quarterback on the Junior team. As Karl moved Joey swerved to the other side, teetering on the platform edge. The man hesitated: if Joey slipped he would be on the electrified rails.

It was all Joey needed. He sprinted for the exit, Karl racing after him.

Suddenly: people, a confusing array of signs, passages and escalators. Escalators. Joey ran up the first he came to, overtaking the people standing on one side, who paid him no attention at all. Karl was only half-a-dozen steps behind him now and gaining.

Joey gave one backward glance, pushed between two protesting women standing on the right and scrambled across the division between the escalator going up and the one going down. He almost slipped but a man on the descending escalator grabbed his arm and Joey half fell, half jumped behind him.

'What's your game?' he said; but Joey was too short of breath to reply.

The man shook his head. 'Kids these days,' he said to no one in particular.

As Joey looked back he could see Karl in a fierce argument with a man in a bowler hat. But he was soon carried away out of sight.

At the bottom of the escalator Joey turned into the first passage he came to, then took another at random until he came to an 'Exit' sign.

He got past the ticket collector by bunching himself in with a crowd of grown-ups: no one seemed to notice him.

Back on the airport concourse he looked around for a British policeman, as instantly recognisable to him as Big Ben, even though he had never seen either of them in reality. As the crowd moved and parted he saw the familiar domed helmet not fifty yards away.

For the third time that day Police Constable MacGuire had a small boy come up to him and say 'I've lost my parents.'

*

Sergeant Goodwin looked at Joey over his glasses.

'You mean to tell me that your parents have been kidnapped and that you were kidnapped as well?'

'That's right,' said Joey, 'they held a gun to my head. And then I escaped from the people who were pretending to be my mother and father. And then another man pretending to be a British agent chased me but I escaped from him.'

Sergeant Goodwin glanced at P.C. MacGuire who raised his eyes to the ceiling. These American kids.

'And just who do you think these kidnappers are?'

'My father's a physicist,' said Joey, 'this other man, the one who was pretending to be my father, is going to take his place. So I guess he's a spy.'

Sergeant Goodwin sat looking at him, saying nothing, and rubbing his chin with the back of his hand.

Joey could feel himself getting irritated.

'Why aren't you doing something?' he asked. 'Why aren't you sending out your men to arrest these people?'

'Why not indeed?' replied the sergeant, frowning at P.C. MacGuire who had a broad grin on his face.

The phone rang on the sergeant's desk: he picked it up.

As he listened he looked at Joey, nodding now and then.

'We've got him here,' he said, 'says he was abducted.'

He listened again and then laughed. 'Did they?' he said.

'About five feet tall, dark curly hair, red sweatshirt, denim jeans and what they call trainers.'

He grunted. 'So that tallies.'

The sergeant put his hand over the mouthpiece.

'Can you describe your parents?'

Joey jumped up.

'Are they all right?'

The sergeant regarded him solemnly. 'I just want to make sure I get you the right set of parents,' he said.

Joey's mind was racing. They must have got away: and then gone straight to the airport police. Just as he had.

'Well, what do they look like?'

Joey told him. He couldn't remember the clothes exactly: they always wore the same kind of things.

Sergeant Goodwin repeated the description over the telephone and then replaced the receiver.

'Your mum and dad'll be here in ten minutes,' he said.

Joey pulled a face and then grinned. 'I'm real sorry if I was rude,' he said, 'I should have known my dad could deal with those kidnappers.'

'Sounds like you're all pretty good at it,' said P.C. MacGuire.

'I think we can do without the benefit of your opinion, MacGuire,' said Sergeant Goodwin. 'If you've nothing better to do you can get this young man a Coke and make me a cup of tea.'

Joey was reading a comic the sergeant had found for him when a policewoman put her head round the door: 'The Medallos are here, to collect their little boy.'

Joey threw down his comic in relief as the door opened.

And then stopped.

'Why, Joey, what a fright you've given us!'

It was the couple he had escaped from in the underground.

FOUR

'They aren't my parents,' said Joey, turning to Sergeant Goodwin, 'these are the kidnappers.'

'Oh, Joey,' said the woman, 'how could you say such a thing!'

'Look, sergeant,' said the man, 'I'm terribly sorry about all this. Joey likes to play these kind of games: I guess he suffers from an over-active imagination. Why, at Kennedy Airport he told customs we were drug smugglers and they searched everything we had.' He lowered his voice. 'I'm afraid we're having a lot of trouble with him.'

'I can believe that,' said Sergeant Goodwin.

'I want you to understand that Joey's a good boy, really,' said the woman, taking Joey's arm, 'it's just that he's got psychological problems.' And she fixed Sergeant Goodwin with a dazzling smile.

'How can you be so dumb?' shouted Joey. But Sergeant Goodwin was unmoved.

'Look, sergeant,' said the man Joey knew as Paul, 'I hope you won't have to go to the trouble of writing reports or anything like that.'

Sergeant Goodwin shook his head. 'If I put all this in the book they'd never believe me.'

Paul laughed.

'Well, I'm sure grateful you've got a sense of humour.'

And he shook the sergeant by the hand.

'Come on Joey, we've got a car waiting outside.'

The woman steered him firmly towards the door. Joey couldn't think what to say: in desperation he kicked out at the woman's legs.

She gave a cry as he caught her on the ankle and for a moment her expression was murderous.

'Joey, how could you do that to your mother!'

Paul took him by the collar, looking back at the sergeant apologetically.

'They've got their hands full with that one,' said Sergeant Goodwin to himself, as Joey and his 'parents' disappeared down the steps. With a sigh he picked up the pile of report forms he had been checking through before Joey had arrived to disturb his peace of mind.

This time they were going by car: there was going to be no chance to repeat the performance.

'You get in the back with him, I'll drive,' said the woman. Her tone made it clear that she was in charge.

'O.K., Louie.'

'And I'm not Louie. I'm Margaret Medallo, your wife and Joey's mother, and don't forget it.'

So she was called 'Louie'; but first names didn't tell you much. And Joey had the feeling that they wouldn't let him hear anything that mattered. But if he was going to stay with them then perhaps sometimes they would forget to be cautious: he would have to keep his eyes and ears open.

Even if he didn't have another chance to escape he might learn something.

The hired car was a Jaguar. The woman drove expertly and fast, though she was careful to keep within the speed limit. Joey could see that she kept an eye on the rear-view mirror; and when they stopped at traffic lights she briefly checked the cars to left and right. The traffic was building up.

Where were they heading? Central London, of course. He knew that an apartment had been rented for him and his parents overlooking Kensington Gardens. A big park with Peter Pan's statue in it, his mother had said. Could they be going there?

Where else? If these two people were taking his parents' place they would have to do everything his parents would have done. Including looking after him: just one big happy family. 'Huh!' Joey laughed out loud and Paul looked at him, mystified.

The woman swung the car round a corner, filtering between a very square-looking black car that must be a London taxi and a red double-decker bus. On the opposite side of the road was a park enclosed by iron railings.

'Almost home, Joey.' It was the first time she had spoken to him since they left the police station.

The car turned into a side road and stopped on the forecourt of a large, modern apartment block.

'Stay where you are,' said Paul as he got out; but when Joey cautiously tried the door on his side it was locked anyway. Childproof locks: what a joke.

A uniformed porter came forward.

'Dr and Mrs Medallo?' he asked, 'we've been expecting you.'

The woman called Louie opened the door on Joey's side and leant towards him. Close to, and unsmiling, her face looked quite different. Not a bit like his mother.

'I want no more tricks,' she said. 'We've made allowances for you up to now, but any more trouble and your parents suffer, is that clear?'

Joey could feel his heart beating. So far he had acted by instinct, he hadn't had time to be really frightened. But he was frightened of this woman; and he knew he had cause to be.

The porter took them up in the lift to the sixth floor, chatting cheerfully in what even Joey recognised as a cockney accent. Louie responded, playing the part of the American tourist. Joey watched her animated face: you would never think she was other than she pretended to be. Except that her eyes were somehow watchful: she was on the alert for something happening.

Paul remained silent and unmoving.

The porter saw them out of the lift and unlocked the door of the apartment, handing Paul the key. But it was Louie who remembered to tip him; and generously.

Joey went in first, his 'parents' following him. As the door slammed and Paul turned the key in the mortice lock Joey realised that he was trapped; or very nearly. Getting out of a sixth floor apartment with only one door wouldn't be easy. Even the porter was like a guard at the entrance: with a £20 note Louie had made him a friend for life.

Paul started to speak but the woman signalled him to be quiet. On a small pad she wrote: 'Check it out'.

Paul nodded, took off his jacket, and started a systematic search of the sitting room, taking down pictures, looking inside vases and under furniture, and behind the radiators.

After just five minutes he shook his head. 'I'll check the other rooms,' he said quietly.

Louie sat down on a sofa and looked up at Joey who stood, stubbornly, in the middle of the carpet.

'Isn't it lovely to be here at last?' she said. The words didn't mean much but on her face was a smile of triumph.

Despite himself Joey felt his eyes filling with tears: he turned angrily away.

FIVE

As he lay in bed that night Joey told himself the whole thing was crazy. Yesterday – it would have been yesterday, even allowing for the time difference – yesterday he had gone to sleep in a New York hotel, with his mother and father in the next room. And tonight he was in London with two strangers who were passing themselves off as his parents.

He didn't know what to do. The more he thought about it the more helpless he felt. At first he had acted on impulse, things just happened: he'd been lucky, then he'd been unlucky. Because he had done the unexpected, the grown-ups had been caught by surprise. But there wasn't much scope for that now; they'd be watching him more carefully.

No, he'd have to plan to beat their plans. But where to start? His mind was just a blank.

What did his father say a scientist did? You start with what you know. From that you try to guess at what you don't know. And then you try to test out your guesses.

If this man Paul was taking his father's place at the research base here in England then he must be a physicist. Nobody else would be able to make sense of it all. Joey had once looked at some of his father's papers that were marked 'Secret and Confidential': he couldn't read most of the words, let alone understand the formulae and mathematics that went with them.

Louie was obviously in charge, so she must be the spy or agent or whatever it was. Perhaps Paul wasn't a spy at all, just a scientist who talked English like an American and looked like his father. It must have been difficult to find someone who would fool the scientists who knew about his father. Not that he'd ever been to the U.K. before, but they must have seen photographs, met him at conferences perhaps.

The whole operation must be a very big thing. That must be where the man called Andersen came in; probably there were many more agents involved than the ones he had seen. And whose side were they on? Andersen didn't look like Joey's idea of a Russian spy.

And what did the 'real' British Intelligence Service know about it? Perhaps nothing at all. Dr and Mrs Medallo and their son Joey had been expected: and they'd arrived.

If only that police sergeant hadn't been so dumb . . .

These people were clever. Louie was clever. She thought of everything: removing the key from Joey's bedroom door, checking that he'd cleaned his teeth. She'd even made sure that he was tucked up in bed, and for a horrible moment he thought she was going to kiss him goodnight.

The whole thing was crazy.

Joey fell asleep . . .

When he woke he realised that he had slept late. Everything was quiet in the apartment and at first Joey thought they might have gone out and left him sleeping. Some hope.

The door of his room opened and Paul looked round.

'Your "mother" has just gone shopping,' he said, without the trace of a smile, 'breakfast's ready when you want it.'

He closed the door before Joey could think of anything to say in reply. Perhaps it wasn't the time to be smart; anyway he was hungry. He scrambled out of bed and started pulling on his clothes.

Joey was still eating his breakfast when the doorbell rang. Paul looked up.

'That's probably Louie,' he muttered, 'stay where you are.'

But Joey didn't need to move: from where he was sitting he could see right through into the hall.

'You've been quick, Louie,' Paul began, as he opened the door; and then he stopped.

The man outside was very tall, and slightly stooping, wearing a long and untidy raincoat. Even his glasses, lopsided on his face, managed to look untidy. He blinked through them.

'My name is Chalmers,' he said, 'Dr Peter Chalmers. You must be Dr Medallo.'

'Dr Medallo' opened the door wider.

'Come in,' he said, 'my wife's just out shopping, this is our son, Joey.'

'Pleased to meet you, Joey.' Dr Chalmers took him by the hand. Joey just nodded, his mouth full of waffle and maple syrup.

'Chalmers,' said Paul thoughtfully, 'I don't know your name but presumably you work with . . .'

'Dr Parkinson. That's right, but he's gone and broken his leg in a skiing accident. I realise I'm second best.' And he smiled apologetically.

'That wasn't what I meant,' said Paul, 'but I thought it was Parkinson who knows all about the process I'm over here to study.'

Dr Chalmers nodded his head which made his hair fall over his eyes. He pushed it back with one hand so that it stood up like a brush.

'I've been working on the project,' he said, 'but I'm no Parkinson, just a run-of-the-mill physicist.'

And he lowered himself onto the sofa, which brought him on a level with Joey.

'How do you like London, Joey?'

'It's O.K.'

'But a bit dull after New York, I expect?'

Joey started to laugh and almost choked.

Paul broke in, eager to interrupt the conversation.

'Joey hasn't had a chance to see anything of London yet; his mother plans to take him round the sights.' He talked quickly, clasping his hands together. In Louie's absence he seemed nervous and unsure of himself.

Dr Chalmers appeared not to notice. He took an envelope out of his pocket.

'I've brought this for you to study, Medallo,' he said, flattening out several sheets of bluish paper with the words MOST SECRET stamped in red at the top. 'You already have security clearance but I'd be glad if you took care of it. Our Russian friends would give a good deal for a glance at this.' And he laughed.

Paul picked the papers up, unable to keep the excitement out of his eyes.

'And this is your security pass, with the photograph you supplied.' Dr Chalmers looked up. 'Not a bad likeness as

things go. You'll need to wear that on a clip at all times. And you'll be finger-printed on the first day: an electronic finger-print check on entering and leaving will be routine after that.'

'Of course, of course,' said Paul hurriedly.

'And a car will collect you every day at 9:30 – if that's convenient?'

Paul nodded, his eyes still on the pages he held in his hands.

Joey watched the two men. You could almost tell what Paul was thinking; but Dr Chalmers' face was – friendly, yet it showed nothing.

The doorbell rang.

Paul put down the papers he was holding, opened the door into the hall and closed it behind him. Joey recognised Louie's voice.

But he wasn't attending to that. He was staring at Dr Chalmers who did two very strange things very quickly.

He picked up the document that Paul had been studying and replaced it with an identical one he took out of his pocket. And then almost in the same movement he reached under the coffee table with a flat disc in his hand, pressed it into place, and then sat back.

He caught Joey's eye and shook his head slightly as the door from the hall opened to admit Louie, laden with shopping.

She turned on her welcoming smile just as if she had pressed a button.

'Well,' she said, 'you're our first visitor.'

Dr Chalmers got to his feet, awkward and confused, not at all like a man who had just switched envelopes and fixed something mysterious underneath the coffee table.

Of course . . . it must be the kind of thing Paul was searching for when they first came to the apartment. A bug, that was it. He had found nothing, and perhaps he wouldn't search again for a while, at least. And if they talked near the coffee table someone would be listening in. British Intelligence must know what had happened after all!

Joey stared at Dr Chalmers: he didn't look a bit like an intelligence agent. Obviously Paul and Louie didn't think so either.

Louie chattered brightly until Dr Chalmers excused himself, saying he had another appointment, and left.

He didn't speak to Joey again, or even look at him. He didn't need to: he had told Joey a great deal.

SIX

If Joey expected something to happen quickly he was disappointed.

Everything seemed to go as Paul and Louie had planned it. Or as Andersen had planned it . . .

An official car called for 'Dr Medallo' every morning at 9:30. And when he came back to the apartment in the evening he seemed well satisfied with the information he was getting. He made long recordings on a miniature tape-recorder and drew detailed sketches which Louie photographed and then burnt.

Most of the recording was done seated on the sofa, with the recorder resting on the coffee table. Joey regularly checked to make sure the bug was still there.

One morning Louie came into the room and almost caught him peering underneath.

'Quit fooling around!' she snapped.

He would have to be careful. If she found the bug she might guess that he had known about it; and what that meant. Louie was sharp.

Every day she took him on a relentless sightseeing tour. The British Museum, Madame Tussaud's, The Tower of London, the Barbican Centre, down the river all the way to

Greenwich, right up into the dome of St Paul's; they missed nothing.

But in all those places, in all those crowds, Joey never had a chance to get away. It was in the waxworks that he first noticed Karl was shadowing them. Other men as well, who changed from day to day. Joey didn't always know who they were but occasionally he would see Karl catch the eye of a man lounging against a wall or nod to a man buying a ticket. Sometimes he noticed that a couple of men would stay with their group as they moved round a museum.

Louie paid them no attention: presumably she knew that they would do their job.

For the first few days Joey had expected a dramatic rescue: police breaking into the apartment or plain-clothes detectives snatching him when they were out on their sightseeing tours.

But there was nothing. In fact, the whole thing was curiously ordinary. Both he and Louie liked milk shakes and they made a point of looking out for places where you could get them. Sometimes he even forgot to be hostile and talked about baseball or a movie they had watched on television.

But if he asked about his parents Louie always gave the same answer: 'You behave yourself, they'll be O.K.'

They ate well and Louie went to some trouble to buy the things he liked.

Paul cooked for all of them, just as Joey's father did at home. And he was really good at it. But sometimes it would come over Joey that it was all wrong and he would get up from the table, leaving his food, and go into his room.

*

32

Nearly ten days passed like this. Joey didn't even admit to himself but at the back of his mind was the feeling that there was some kind of hitch, that things weren't working out. . .

And what about Dr Chalmers? From what Paul said most of his time was spent with him. And in the last couple of days he had begun to say that some things were being held back from him.

'Be patient,' Louie had said, 'you're getting close to what really matters. They're bound to be cautious.'

But if it was difficult for Paul to be patient, for Joey it was even more so.

The British were doing nothing; absolutely nothing. He had to help himself, do something. But how? He was virtually a prisoner there.

Joey wandered out onto the balcony: he often did that, there was quite a view. Louie did no more than glance at him.

He leant over the railings and looked down. Nothing compared with a skyscraper but it was sixty feet all the same. There was no escaping that way.

Joey turned to go back into the sitting room. And then stopped as the idea came into his head.

Maybe he couldn't go down, but what about up? They were on the top floor. The apartment block had a flat roof, you could see that much; and there must be some way of getting down from there.

He looked up: about fifteen feet to the edge of the parapet. He examined the wall. No drainpipes near. But . . . there was a pattern in the brickwork made up of yellowish half-bricks

33

jutting out from the red-brick walls. Not all over – in a kind of zig-zag. And they ran right up to the parapet. Could he climb up there?

It made him sweat just to think of it. Each brick jutted out about four inches.

If he stood on the edge of the balcony, he would just be able to reach one of the yellow bricks. And if he was careful . . . And if he wasn't? There was a drop of sixty feet.

Joey went back into the sitting room. His heart was thumping and his face felt hot. He had to act normally.

Louie was reading a magazine and smoking a cigarette. It had to be done as soon as possible, before he had too much time to think about it. There was this horrible picture in his head where he could see himself falling and falling . . .

Joey picked up a book and forced himself to read. He could hear the faint rustling noise as Louie turned over the pages of her magazine.

He needed just a few minutes with Louie out of the way. Didn't she ever need to go to the bathroom like normal people?

He kept reading the same page again and again.

Louie stood up and stubbed out her cigarette.

'I'm just going to take a shower,' she said, 'then we'll go out.'

Joey nodded, frowning over his book.

The bathroom door clicked shut.

Joey counted to twenty slowly in his head in case she came out again for something she'd forgotten.

' . . . nineteen, twenty.'

He put down his book and moved across to the balcony, careful to make no noise.

34

Without hesitating he climbed up onto the balcony railings. *He couldn't do it*; he scrambled down again, trembling. It was crazy, it wasn't worth it . . .

He was wasting time. He swung himself up again. The nearest brick was only a foot away. He leant forward and grasped it. No going back now. First one foot then the other. For a moment his second foot couldn't find the brick that was there, just empty space.

Don't panic.

His left hand was pressed against the wall, holding on to nothing. He reached up and grabbed a brick above his head. Now there was nothing between him and the pavement sixty feet below except those four half-bricks – and air.

He knew a bit about rock-climbing. Two hands and two feet: four points on the surface. And you only moved one at a time.

Easier said than done. He was stuck like a fly on a wall. He couldn't bring himself to move his hold. But he had to.

Joey lifted his left foot onto the brick above, then his right hand.

One foot up, one hand up. Keep going, *keep going*.

One foot up, one hand up. It was going on for ever. His fingers were feeling numb, he was gripping so hard.

Just keep going, all he had to do was keep going.

He glanced up: the edge of the parapet was no more than six feet away.

It was then that he made his mistake. He lifted his left foot and grabbed for a brick with his right hand at the same time; it came away in his hand as he pulled.

He swung outwards from the wall, the brick grazing his shoulder as it fell.

He couldn't hold just with his left hand: he was going to fall.

With a sob of fear he swung himself back towards the wall and rammed his right fist into the hole where the brick had come loose.

Joey closed his eyes: he couldn't move, couldn't think. He needed a minute, just a minute . . .

Now!

Four quick movements and he was scrambling over the parapet. He collapsed onto the flat roof, spreading himself wide: it was good to have something solid underneath you. For a few seconds he just lay there.

But there was no time to waste: he pulled himself up into a kneeling position and looked around. Not five yards away was a door: it must open on to the staircase.

He dashed across and turned the handle. Locked. He pulled and twisted at it but it was useless.

What else? To one side of the door was a skylight, over the stairwell, no doubt; and on one side it was half open.

He looked through. He would have to be careful. If he missed the stairs he would . . . well, he'd been lucky once.

Joey wriggled through without difficulty and swung his legs in the direction of the stairs as he let go.

He hit the bannister with his back and rolled down a flight of stairs. The noise was terrific.

He picked himself up and listened: nothing. Nobody came running.

Carefully, a step at a time, and listening after every step, Joey drew nearer to the landing outside the apartment. After the next turn in the stairs he would be there.

How long had it all taken? Minutes, even though it

seemed like hours. Almost certainly Louie was still in the bathroom.

He'd done it!

But as he turned the last corner he saw that the landing wasn't empty. Karl was there, leaning against the wall, on guard. And there was no getting past him this time.

The one worthwhile thing in the whole episode was the sight of Louie's face as she opened the apartment door, clutching her bathrobe, her wet hair plastered across her face.

For once she had nothing to say.

SEVEN

It was raining hard. Sightseeing was out of the question and Joey felt there couldn't be much else left to see.

Louie was teaching him to play patience. As she laid out the cards she shivered.

'It's getting cold in here,' she said, 'I'll turn the heating up.'

She put her hand on the radiator.

'It's almost cold, no wonder we're feeling it!'

She rang down to the porter who said he would get a heating engineer to come right away.

Louie put on a jacket that was hanging in the hall.

'You'd better get yourself a sweater,' she told Joey.

Joey obeyed: arguing with Louie was never worth the trouble.

The heating engineer arrived as promptly as the porter had promised.

He was a small, rather plump man with a bald head and a permanently cheerful expression. And he talked all the time.

'The trouble with you Americans,' he said, 'is that you're too used to all this central heating. Hot-house, that's what you are.'

'Yes, yes,' said Louie in the tone of voice she sometimes used with Paul, 'just fix the heating.'

'Don't you worry, lady,' said the little man, lighting himself a cigarette, 'there's nothing I can't fix.'

Louie, barely concealing her irritation, went through into the kitchen leaving the door open.

'Here,' said the man to Joey, 'you hold this spanner and my fags while I try and shift this valve.'

Joey grinned: he liked the man because he obviously didn't mind Louie's off-hand manner.

But as he looked down at the open cigarette packet in his hand his grin faded. On the flap was written this message: 'When the doorbell rings *dot-dot-dash-dot-dot* go into your bedroom, shut the door and put a towel along the bottom of the door.'

Joey closed the packet, his mind suddenly very alert. He wasn't quite sure what the message meant. Except that when the doorbell went in that kind of morse pattern he had to get out of the way very quickly. Perhaps there was going to be shooting? But what about the towel?

He looked at the heating engineer, lying on his side on the carpet, pulling at the stuck valve with a wrench.

'Success!' he said at last, sitting up. 'I think I deserve another smoke for that.' And he took the packet of cigarettes out of Joey's hands.

Joey watched him: he really was very ordinary-looking.

Louie came back in from the kitchen.

'Any time your lad wants a job,' said the irrepressible little man, 'just give me a ring. He's got patience, and the important thing in my job is to have patience.'

'I'm running out of it myself,' said Louie, tight-lipped,

40

'have you fixed the heating?'

'You won't have no more problems, lady,' said the man, 'you can take that coat off now.'

He gathered up his tools, whistling through his teeth as he did so.

'See you!' he said, waving his hand.

Louie scowled after him.

The door slammed: the heating engineer had gone. If he *was* a heating engineer.

When the doorbell rang later that afternoon Joey was ready for it.

Dot-dot-dash it went.

Joey got to his feet. But it stopped there. Joey hesitated, puzzled.

Louie opened the door. It was Andersen: the man Joey had seen at Heathrow. The man in charge.

That Andersen was someone very important was immediately obvious from Louie's manner towards him.

'I didn't expect you,' she said nervously.

Andersen didn't reply but advanced on Joey like an uncle who had caught sight of a favourite nephew.

'Well, Joey,' he said, 'have you planned any more escapes?'

Joey looked defiant and said nothing.

Andersen pulled a face and laughed.

'So you're mad at me; I understand. If I was you I would be mad at me. Here, look what I brought you.'

He pulled out of his coat-pocket a box of Hershey bars, the kind with roasted almonds in: Joey's favourite.

'How did you know I liked those?'

Andersen lifted his hands in mock surprise.

'Don't you know Andersen knows everything?'

Despite himself, Joey grinned.

Andersen took off his coat and settled himself in an armchair. 'That's better. O.K., so we are enemies, but we can still enjoy a joke, eh?'

He broke one of the chocolate bars and gave Joey half.

'Your parents said to buy you these. I saw them yesterday and they're O.K. Everybody's O.K. So long as they do what Andersen says.'

Louie stood respectfully by his chair. 'Can I get you a drink, Comrade Andersen?'

He roared with laughter, slapping his leg.

'Comrade Andersen,' he mimicked, 'what sort of talk is that? Comrade Joey and I will have a Coke while I show him a few tricks.'

He took a 10p piece out of his pocket and gave it to Joey; then he spread his hands, wide apart.

'Put the coin in one of my hands,' he said.

Joey dropped it onto the broad palm of his right hand. Andersen closed his fists.

'O.K.,' he said, 'I'm going to put my hands flat down on the table and I bet you can't tell which hand the coin is under.'

Joey watched carefully: 'I'll bet you a Hershey bar,' he said.

Andersen slapped both hands down onto the coffee table. Joey winced: he'd forgotten about the bug underneath. But nothing fell down.

'Which hand?'

Joey touched the right one. Andersen turned it over: it was empty. Then he turned over the left hand: empty. The coin had disappeared.

'So what do you learn?'

Joey shook his head.

Andersen's smile slipped for a moment.

'You learn that Andersen knows all the tricks and wins all the tricks. Little ones and big ones.'

As Andersen watched him Joey felt himself go cold. Could Andersen know anything? You felt as if he was the kind of man you couldn't hide things from.

Andersen laughed again.

'So, we are too serious. I'll show you another trick.'

But Joey's mind wasn't on it. Louie was sharp. But Andersen was a great deal sharper.

Andersen stayed until Paul came home.

They went into one of the other rooms to talk. Louie switched on the television, turned up the sound and pretended to watch. But Joey knew it was so that he couldn't overhear. And the bug wouldn't be able to overhear either.

When the two men came back into the sitting room Andersen was his usual smiling self but somehow alert and wary. Paul looked pale, with the air of a man who had tried to justify himself and failed.

'Tell me, Louie,' said Andersen in a quiet voice that sounded like a threat, 'have there been any unexpected visitors here, anybody at all?'

There was a moment's silence.

'Who?' pressed Andersen.

'The central heating broke down . . .' she began and then stopped.

'And an engineer came to fix it?'

43

Andersen looked from one to the other.

'A trick as old as that and you fell for it?'

'But, Comrade Andersen!'

He ignored her and turned to Paul.

'Search the place. Thoroughly.'

Andersen sat on the sofa, quite still. Louie didn't take her eyes off him. She looked ill. Ill and frightened.

Paul worked quickly and carefully.

Nobody spoke.

Perhaps because Andersen was sitting there Paul came to the sofa and coffee table last of all.

'I beg your pardon, Comrade Andersen.'

Andersen got up without a word, waited until Paul had finished searching the sofa, and then sat down again.

Paul turned the coffee table over in one swift movement, and then stopped. And pointed.

Andersen nodded heavily.

Paul fetched a bucket of water from the kitchen, detached the bug and dropped it in.

'Come here, Joey.'

Joey went and stood in front of Andersen.

'Did you know about this?'

Joey didn't feel scared but he knew that Andersen wasn't someone you could lie to.

'I know the heating engineer didn't put it there. I held his cigarettes and his spanner; but he didn't go anywhere near the coffee-table.'

'That's right,' said Louie eagerly, 'I could hear what was going on and could see most of it.'

'But it wasn't there when we arrived: I'd swear to it.' Paul's hands were shaking.

Andersen raised his eyebrows.

'So who put it there? Joey?'

'But nobody else has been here!' Louie exclaimed.

'Is that quite correct?' Andersen sounded like a teacher dealing with a not-very-bright-pupil.

Paul put his hand on the back of a chair to steady himself.

'Nobody except Peter Chalmers,' he said.

'Nobody except Peter Chalmers,' Andersen went on, pointing the lesson, 'Dr Peter Chalmers who has been feeding you with a lot of information about as secret as a railway timetable and probably a good deal less accurate.'

Paul sat down, his shoulders hunched forward.

'But when?' Louie had recovered her confidence, clear now that the fault wasn't hers.

Paul lifted his head, not daring to look at Andersen.

'When I answered the door.'

Andersen spoke: very quietly. 'Did you see Dr Chalmers do it, Joey?'

'Yes.' There was no point in lying.

Andersen rubbed his hands together, slowly.

'You know what I think? I think Joey is brighter than either of you. With Joey on my side I would win. With you two, I lose.'

Joey's heart was beating so loud he could almost hear it.

Andersen took hold of Joey's hands and looked in his face. 'Joey, when this heating engineer came, what did he tell you?'

Joey knew what to do now. You didn't lie but you didn't tell all the truth, either.'

'He told me to be patient.'

'Anything else?'

'He said I could have a job with him.'

Andersen patted his shoulder; then his face hardened.

'You will all leave at mid-day tomorrow. You, Paul, will be too ill to go to the laboratory in the morning. Do you understand?'

'Comrade Andersen . . .'

Andersen stopped him with a glance.

'Save your explanations,' he said, 'for Moscow.'

EIGHT

The doorbell went just as Joey was going to the bathroom the next morning.

Dot-dot-dash-dot-dot.

He almost turned and went back to his bedroom, as instructed. No, it would look more natural to keep going.

Paul was still in his dressing-gown, drinking coffee.

'Answer the door!' Louie called from the kitchen. 'It'll be the chauffeur; you'll have to tell him you're not going today.'

Joey slipped into the bathroom and bolted the door. There were no windows and a ventilator came on automatically as you pulled the light switch. A towel. He took a damp one off the towel rail and stuffed it firmly across the crack at the bottom of the door. He had an idea why that might be important.

Then he stood quietly, listening.

For a few seconds there was nothing. Then a shout of protest: Paul's voice. Then other voices and three muffled thumps followed by a faint hissing noise like a bicycle tyre going down.

A distant scream, somebody calling out and then the sound of coughing and choking. There was a thud as someone fell against the bathroom door and tried the

handle, followed by the crash of overturning furniture, of glass shattering, the kind of noises that Joey associated with bar-room fights in Westerns.

There was a strange smell and Joey felt his eyes smarting; his throat hurt. He pushed the towel more tightly against the door with his foot.

But it got worse: his eyes and nose were running, it hurt him to breathe.

Outside things were almost quiet: he could just hear

someone moving around. But he made no move to open the door. Safer to stay where he was.

There came a tap on the door.

D*ot-dot-dash-dot-dot.*

Joey pulled away the towel, unbolted the door and opened it.

And then fell back, coughing and spluttering, as the CS gas was drawn into the bathroom.

A man with goggles and a face-mask picked him up and rushed across the room to the small balcony that overlooked the park.

Joey leant over the railing, gasping for breath.

The man pulled off his goggles and mask: it was Dr Chalmers.

'Well done,' he said.

Fifteen minutes later the sitting room was almost clear of the gas, but it was as if a bomb had hit it. Furniture was overturned, a window was smashed and what looked like coffee had been thrown against the wall.

A man dressed in a kind of black tracksuit came in as 'Dr Chalmers' was explaining things to Joey.

'You got them away then, sergeant?'

'Yes, sir,' said the man, fingering a scratch across his face.

Joey could imagine how he got that.

'Are you police?' he asked.

'I'm MI6 – counter-intelligence, the sergeant is SAS.'

'So you're not a physicist?'

'Well, I am, as a matter of fact. Not in the same league as your father, of course.'

Joey looked at him. 'What about my father? My mom. What's happened to them?'

'The plan is that your parents will be snatched from where they're being kept, ten minutes after we rescue you. I know what you're thinking: why did we wait until now? It's true we could have picked up the other two any time, but we wanted a lead on Andersen: he's the big one. We've had to plan carefully and time things to the minute.'

'So my parents have been rescued by now?'

'I expect a phone call any second; literally any second.'

For the first time in the whole episode Joey felt tears coming to his eyes and he couldn't blame the CS gas. He turned away and went into his bedroom to get dressed.

It was another fifteen minutes before the phone rang. Joey sat on the edge of his bed, waiting. Although the door was closed he could hear every sound in the next room.

Chalmers didn't say much as he took the call; for the first two or three minutes he just listened.

'What sort of a start did they have on you, do you think?'

Silence.

'As long as that?'

Silence again; but Joey could imagine an anxious voice on the other end of the line. *Something had gone wrong.*

'No, they couldn't possibly have been warned from here.'

A click as the phone went down.

Joey opened the bedroom door.

Chalmers was standing by the telephone, staring down at the floor.

'They were too quick for us,' he said, without looking up,

'they got away with your parents before my men even arrived.'

It hit Joey like a blow: he felt too numb to be angry.

'It was Andersen,' said Joey, 'he always knows more than you ever think he knows.'

Even as he stood there the phone rang again.

Chalmers signalled to him to pick it up.

'Joey?' It was Andersen's voice.

'Where's my mom and dad?'

'Safe. Safe and sound: you know you can trust me. I should like to speak to Dr Chalmers.'

Without a word Joey handed him the receiver.

'Chalmers speaking.'

'And this is Colonel Andrei Andersen of the KGB: we know about each other. You have in your custody my two rather inept colleagues; I have Dr and Mrs Medallo. I suggest we do a straight swap.'

'In return for what?'

'You let us leave the country without any fuss.'

'I don't have authority for that.'

'Then get it.'

The line went dead.

Chalmers put the phone down, slowly.

It was Andersen's game.

NINE

The hands on Big Ben stood at five minutes to five.

Westminster Bridge was crowded with vehicles and pedestrians streaming north and south across the river: the evening rush hour.

On the north side of the bridge three unmarked cars were parked near the Houses of Parliament on double yellow lines. But no traffic police approached them. In two of the cars a man and a woman sat in the back seat, each wedged between a couple of solid-looking men who appeared out of place in civilian clothes. Paul seemed on edge, as usual, but Louie had a half-smile on her face.

In the third car Joey sat with Chalmers. He wasn't sure what it was all about, but they were here at Andersen's request: he knew that much.

They were silent as the minute hand of Big Ben crept towards the hour.

Five o'clock had just begun to strike when the call sign came up on the car radio. The driver picked up the handset, had difficulty in hearing as Big Ben boomed out.

'For you, sir.' He passed the handset across to Chalmers.

'Andersen speaking.'

'Go ahead.'

'At 5:15 exactly I want you to set my two colleagues walking across the bridge on the left-hand pavement; at the same time we shall release Dr and Mrs Medallo on the south side so that they cross over midway. You will be able to see them – a straight swap like I suggested. Agreed?'

'We have no choice and you know it.'

Andersen laughed.

'Yes,' he said, 'I do know it, and *you* know there must be no tricks, or . . .'

'You don't need to spell it out.'

'Then we are clear on that. Now I should like to speak to Joey.'

Chalmers gave him the handset and showed him how to work the switch. Joey put it to his ear.

'Joey? This is a complicated business, but you have to trust me. If our friend from MI6 is sensible no one will get hurt, do you understand?'

'I want my mom and dad back.'

'Joey, I can promise you a happy ending; but we're not quite there.'

'But this is your country,' protested Joey, 'why don't you just arrest him?'

'It's not as simple as that, Joey,' Chalmers sounded weary, 'we don't know where he is, he's probably on the move all the time. In any case we couldn't arrest him if we didn't have your parents; and we've had one fiasco.'

'And you'll have my parents in a few minutes, then you *can* arrest him.'

'If we can catch him; and we've been trying to do just that for a long time.'

'Isn't there *anything* you can do?'

Chalmers hesitated: 'We've got something he doesn't know about, something we would only use as a last resort. We aren't beaten yet.'

Joey didn't say any more. They would have managed things better in the States. As for Andersen; you couldn't help admiring him. The way he was playing it you would think this was Moscow, not London.

Chalmers went on: 'I've got men watching the south side of the bridge, but we've no idea how your parents will be brought there. Andersen will know we'll be watching and he'll have his own men on the lookout. There are probably some in the crowds on the bridge or driving vans, all looking perfectly normal.'

Joey glanced up: it was a minute to 5:15.

Chalmers raised his hand. The rear doors of the other cars opened and Paul and Louie were helped out, each hand-cuffed to one of their guards.

The minute hand on Big Ben shifted to a quarter past the hour.

Almost to the second their call-sign came up again on the radio.

'It's Wilkinson, sir. A taxi has just dropped two people answering to the description of Dr and Mrs Medallo on the south side, right-hand pavement: they have started to walk across.'

'Are they O.K.?'

'They look pretty scared to me.'

'Don't go near them. Tail the taxi but don't stop it until we confirm that the Medallos are safely in our hands.'

Wilkinson repeated the order.

Chalmers got out of the car and nodded to the guards, who unlocked the handcuffs.

He looked at the two prisoners. 'When I give you the word you start walking across the bridge. Don't run and don't attempt to stop Dr and Mrs Medallo; pace yourself so that you can pass them at about mid-point.'

He paused.

'Now!'

Paul started forward. Joey saw Louie take his arm to restrain him.

Joey leant over the back of the front seat and peered through the windscreen, eager for the first glimpse of his parents. The pavements were crowded. He kept watching.

They came into view quite suddenly through a gap in the crowd. Too far away, though, to make out their faces and he didn't recognise the clothes they were wearing. The gap closed and he lost sight of them.

Paul and Louie had almost reached mid-way. They were hurrying, his parents must be very near. Yes, there was his father's dark, curly hair over-topping the people around him. He must have seen him because he waved.

What happened next all took place very quickly.

Joey couldn't bear just to sit there. He leapt out of the car and ran forward.

Chalmers turned. 'Joey! Wait!'

But he ignored Chalmers' call. He had to get to them. In the midst of the mass of people he couldn't see far ahead. Any second now . . .

He caught a glimpse of their clothes, the crowd parted . . .

It wasn't them. It wasn't his parents.

Joey stopped, puzzled and uncertain as the couple swept past him.

Was it a trick or had he just been looking at the wrong people?

Traffic on the bridge was almost at a standstill. But from

behind he could hear a motor-cycle engine, coming nearer.

He turned to look: perhaps it was the police. No, one of those express delivery motor-cyclists dressed all in black, with a black helmet and visor. He was weaving in and out of the now stationary cars and vans.

The motorcyclist stopped next to him.

'I'm taking you to your parents: jump on behind. Quick!'

Joey obeyed without thinking, grabbing hold of the man's waist as the motor-bike lurched away.

Faster now, the bike swayed from side to side as the man flung it through the gaps in the traffic.

Clear of the bridge the gaps were wider and they raced ahead. Then, without warning, and with a swerve that almost threw Joey off, the man turned into a side-road.

'Hold on!' he shouted.

They roared down a cobbled road, the bike bouncing uncontrollably, then down an alley between warehouses, so narrow that a car couldn't have followed them. Left into a turn so sharp that they skidded, through a tunnel-like arch, the exhaust booming and reverberating. Now to the right up an unmade track littered with debris, bricks, broken glass. It looked deserted and yet here they were in central London, not far from the river. Joey had no idea in which direction they were going but the motor-cyclist seemed to have an exact map in his head: he didn't hesitate once.

They skirted a scrap metal yard, piled high with rusting cars and other things that Joey couldn't even guess at. Out onto a service road behind what appeared to be run-down shops. The motor-cyclist stopped beside a large pair of garage doors and switched off the engine. It was suddenly very quiet.

'Don't try anything,' he said to Joey and kicked at the doors with one heavy boot. Joey looked around: he wouldn't have known where to run to, anyway.

After a couple of minutes one of the garage doors opened a fraction and a face appeared: it was the blond man Joey had last seen at the airport. The man with the gun. He grunted and opened the door wide, locking it behind them.

Seated on a bench, eating a sandwich, was Andersen dressed in a chauffeur's uniform; a peaked cap lay on the bench beside him. He waved his sandwich at Joey in greeting.

It was quite dark in the garage but as his eyes got accustomed to the light Joey saw that Karl was also there leaning against the wall, smoking a cigarette.

Andersen gestured towards Karl and the blond man: 'These two are anxious to get away.'

'It's a tricky game,' said Karl.

'Sure,' said Andersen and finished his sandwich.

He stood up and dusted himself down, putting on his peaked cap with exaggerated care.

'Your car is ready.' And he inclined his head towards the darker end of the garage where Joey could just make out a gleaming silver-grey Rolls Royce.

Joey walked towards it. Beautiful: the sort of car that always had a chauffeur.

He ran his fingers across the shining coachwork, opened the rear door and smelt the leather upholstery.

Andersen was paying off the motorcyclist, Joey heard the heavy garage doors opening and closing again.

And then silence, an unusual silence. He turned round.

The blond man was standing with his back to the garage

doors and he had a gun in his hand.

And it was pointing at Andersen. To one side Karl stood with his hands in the air, very still.

Andersen nodded slowly.

'So: a double agent. That explains a great deal.'

The blond man ignored him. 'Joey, come here!'

At first Joey couldn't make out what was happening: he hesitated.

'You won't get away with it.' Andersen raised his voice. 'Put that gun down.'

'Joey! Quick!' The blond man moved his head slightly, but without taking his eyes off Andersen.

Joey started forward and then stopped: behind the man the garage doors were opening slowly.

'Look out!'

The blond man wheeled round as Louie fired once; and then again as he tried to lift his gun.

The man pitched forward onto the floor and lay quite still.

'Just in time!' Louie's voice showed her satisfaction; her face even more so. Louie was pleased with herself: her other mistakes would be forgotten now.

Paul, scared and white-faced, slipped through the door behind her; no one paid him any attention.

The blond man was dead: even Joey realised that.

And in that moment he realised something else: that the dead man had been Chalmers' 'last resort'. And he wouldn't even know that it had failed.

TEN

'They're just a couple of look-alikes, snatched on their way to work this morning. They don't know a thing.'

Chalmers glanced across at Joey's 'parents', who were sitting in the police car, and then back to the sergeant who had questioned them.

'So what did they think it was all about?'

'Terrorists. They were told that they would be shot if they didn't obey instructions exactly: to walk across the bridge and to start waving at mid-point.'

Chalmers' voice revealed nothing of how he felt: 'What about the two we released?'

'They vanished. My guess is they got into a van on the bridge and were driven away before the traffic snarled up. And that was a put-up job if ever I saw one: a truck breaking down in the worst possible place. But we'll never prove it.'

Chalmers nodded and turned away. They had been outplayed. It had been a brilliant operation, especially the gamble that Joey would somehow manage to run forward to meet his parents. They had had a plan for everything.

The only hope now lay in the unsuspected double agent, whom he knew as Taylor, but who went by a very different name for the Russians.

*

They had been driving for half-an-hour and nobody had said a word. They were nervous: Joey could sense it. All except Andersen, of course.

He turned and watched him: Andersen was smiling to himself. Yet he could have been dead by now. Did nothing ever worry him?

'Why didn't you pick an ordinary car and why are you all dressed up as a chauffeur?' asked Joey.

'Because everybody notices a chauffeur-driven Rolls but nobody is curious about it. It's too respectable.'

'Quit talking,' said Louie, 'my head aches.'

The car was slowing down. Signs came up saying SERVICES. They were turning off. Were they going to stay here? Back home he sometimes stayed in motels with his parents. Did they have motels in England?

The car park was full of cars that all looked vaguely alike to Joey. But as Andersen reversed the Rolls carefully into a gap he recognised the car next to them: a Cadillac. His grandfather had one just like it.

Andersen took off his chauffeur's cap and turned to face the three of them in the back. He held out some car keys.

'You take the blue Ford over there; Karl drives.' he pointed.

'The three of us together?' Louie sounded doubtful.

Andersen nodded. 'The boy travels with me.'

Louie seemed as if she were going to protest; but in the end she said nothing.

Joey looked across at the car Andersen had pointed to: it was like no Ford he had ever seen.

'The money,' said Karl, 'what about the money?'

62

'I will bring it to you in a moment. Go and check the car first.'

Joey watched them go.

During the car journey Joey's feet had been resting on a small black case, which Andersen now lifted up. Joey knew what was in it: banknotes made up into bundles of £500, and there were dozens of them. He had seen Andersen give four of the bundles to the motor-cyclist in the garage, who had checked them carefully, without saying a word.

Now Andersen took out twenty of the bundles and snapped a rubber band round them: £10,000.

He balanced the notes in his hand. 'See,' he said, 'an agent's main tool is not a gun or secret codes or any of that stuff. It is money: with money you can do anything.'

Andersen reset the combination lock on the case and slid out of his seat.

'Remember, no tricks.'

Joey didn't answer directly.

'Where's my mom and dad? When will I see them?'

'Tomorrow, about mid-day; if all goes well.'

'And what does that mean?'

Andersen lowered his voice. 'It means that if I am safe other people are safe.'

'So you come first!'

Andersen looked at him steadily, and there was an edge to his words: 'You'd better not forget it.'

Joey watched while Andersen walked across to the Ford without any attempt to conceal the money he was holding in his hands. Joey understood: there was never anything suspicious about Andersen, he always looked as though he was doing something that was perfectly all right.

Andersen had given the money to Karl with only a few words. Now he was bending down at the rear window talking to Paul and Louie who were listening intently.

Joey thought: they mustn't get away with it.

Here they were, changing cars, leaving no trail behind.

And he was the only link. The blond man, whatever his name was, was dead. Only he could stop them now.

Karl had started the engine of the other car. Andersen had straightened up, was turning to walk back to the Rolls.

The Rolls was an automatic. Like American cars. You turned on the ignition, put the lever into DRIVE and pressed the accelerator.

Joey did just that. The Rolls shot forward, narrowly missing Andersen as he leapt to one side, and rammed the Ford that Karl was driving.

It sounded like an explosion; there was a moment's stunned silence then – people running, a lot of shouting.

Paul was leaning forward, blood streaming from his head.

Joey was scared but triumphant: he'd stopped them.

Andersen pulled open the off-side door, pushed Joey across to the front passenger seat, and turned off the ignition. He looked dangerous.

'Stay where you are, don't move – or you will never see your parents again. Understood?' He slammed the car door.

'My fault,' said Andersen to the people who clustered round, 'I left my engine running. I hope my friend's all right.'

Louie was dabbing Paul's head with her scarf.

'It's nothing,' she said, 'just a little cut.' Paul didn't look so convinced.

Joey watched it all from inside the car. People had started

moving away: it wasn't so exciting after all. No one really injured and no one arguing.

Then Joey saw Andersen's expression change.

A motorcycle cop was walking in their direction.

As he he came up to them he didn't speak at first, just stood looking at the scene, slowly and carefully: he would remember what he saw.

'Anyone injured?'

'My husband has a small cut on his head, that's all.' Louie gave him one of her dazzling smiles which had no effect at all.

'Can I see your driving licence, sir?'

Andersen produced it from an inside pocket.

The policeman took his time looking it over, then handed it back without a word.

'Perhaps you'd tell me what happened, sir?'

Andersen gave a clear account, with just the right note of embarrassment and apology. He didn't mention Joey.

The policeman took out his notebook but didn't open it. He weighed it in his hand, not hurrying himself.

Joey wanted to get out of the car and run to the policeman. Just two seconds it would take. But he daren't: Andersen meant what he said. It was too terrible to think about.

The policeman put his notebook away and zipped up his jacket.

'If this had occurred on a public highway you could be charged with a motoring offence.'

Andersen nodded.

'But as no one is injured . . . just be careful in future not to leave the car with the engine running, and I suggest you get that gearbox checked.'

The relief on Andersen's face was real enough. 'I'm very grateful: this could have cost me my job!'

Exactly the right thing to say: the policeman half-smiled.

'A hard man your boss, eh?'

'Very hard.'

Andersen sounded as though he meant it.

ELEVEN

They were driving along in one of the smallest cars Joey had ever seen. Andersen had left his chauffeur's cap and jacket on the front seat of the Rolls Royce and had put on a sweater. Joey sat in the front seat next to him.

'Just like father and son,' said Andersen, friendly as ever.

Joey pulled a face at that but he knew what Andersen meant: they looked the part. In fact, Andersen had the knack of always looking the part he played. Even the small, family car – called a Metro – was right. It wasn't the sort of thing you would associate with a secret agent.

'You think you're so smart!'

Andersen didn't respond immediately.

'Do you know what I think, Joey? If anybody is going to outsmart me in this business, it will be you.'

Joey couldn't help being pleased by that; but he wasn't going to show it.

'Andersen: that doesn't sound a very Russian name to me.'

Andersen changed down and overtook a slow, lumbering lorry.

'You're quite right: it is Danish. My father was a Danish sailor: tall and blond and handsome. His ship was torpedoed during the war against Germany; I can hardly remember him. I am short and dark and stocky like my mother. She was a good Russian and a good Communist. I try to be like her.'

'Aren't you married?'

'To my job. I am away most of the time and I cannot say where I am going: no wife would put up with it.'

Joey thought about that.

'Aren't you ever lonely?'

Andersen looked surprised. 'No,' he said, 'I have a lot of friends. They think I do this or that job; friends don't need to know too much.'

He shrugged his shoulders as if to say: that was enough of talking.

It was getting dark but he continued to drive the little car as fast as it would go.

Joey must have fallen asleep because the next thing he knew it was very much darker.

The car had stopped: perhaps that's what had woken him. And as he opened his eyes he could scarcely believe what he saw. In the glare of the headlights, no more than ten yards away, police-cars were blocking the road.

Beside him Andersen sat smoking unconcernedly.

'What's going on?' asked Joey.

'A little way ahead the police have stopped a car, a blue Ford with a damaged nearside door. They expect trouble so it is a big operation.'

'How . . .?' Joey began.

'That policeman was no fool. He must have reported the incident: someone higher up would have been on the look-

out for anything out of the ordinary. All the police in the
country are searching for you and your parents.' Andersen
paused. 'And for me.'

The traffic started moving again. A policeman was waving
them on: they had to pull round the dozen or so police-cars
that still blocked one side of the road, surrounding the blue
Ford that had pulled into the verge.

Only for a moment Joey saw it. Karl was facing the car, his

arms spread out on the roof as a policeman searched him. Louie's face, contorted with anger, showed for a split second in their headlights. She couldn't have seen them, but Joey had an uneasy feeling that she was looking straight at him.

They drove into the darkness leaving the blue flashing lights behind.

'Aren't you going to help them?'

'There is nothing I can do.'

Joey thought for a minute. 'You *knew* the police would catch up with them because they knew about their car; they didn't know about this one.'

'They made a mistake: they should have abandoned the car.'

'Don't you ever make a mistake?' Joey meant it to be sarcastic but it came out just like a question.

'Clever or stupid, everyone makes mistakes,' said Andersen, 'but the clever man knows what to do about them.'

Joey turned that over in his mind. Andersen had made mistakes: perhaps he would make one too many.

He didn't feel sleepy any more.

They had passed a town called Basingstoke a while ago; and he had just seen a sign for a place called Winchester.

Where were they heading for?

'Southampton,' said Andersen, breaking in on his thoughts. 'A kind of bed and breakfast accommodation has been arranged for us: no registers to sign. Supper too, if you are a good boy.'

'And then what?'

'There is a Soviet freighter loading in Southampton docks: it sails tomorrow morning. I shall be joining it.'

Joey looked at him. 'What about me?'

'I shall be leaving you where you can be collected – like a parcel.'

TWELVE

The last sign had said: Southampton 6 miles.

Andersen seemed to know exactly where he was going. Not once did he stop to consult a map or to ask the way. He didn't even seem to pay any attention to the road signs.

They were in the centre of the town now: nothing but shops and offices. Where on earth were they going to stay?

Andersen took a left turn and slowed down outside a row of new shop units with a TO LET sign over them. He turned left into a service road and then left again. They were at the back of the shop units which were securely boarded, each with a heavy wooden door.

Andersen got out of the car and, taking a large key from his pocket, unlocked one of the doors. It swung open, but you could see nothing of what was inside.

Joey was so curious it didn't even occur to him that he might have made a run for it.

'Are we going to sleep *here?*'

What Andersen did always made you want to ask questions.

'I have slept in worse places.'

He took Joey by the arm and pushed him through the

doorway, locking the door after them. It was completely dark: Joey couldn't see a thing.

Andersen switched on a pencil torch: even that narrow beam he kept low.

The shop unit was quite bare: concrete and breeze blocks and wooden battens. And empty except for two large cardboard boxes stacked tidily in one corner.

Andersen squatted down beside the boxes, his back to Joey.

'Here are sleeping bags and food and drink,' he said.

He emptied the boxes carefully, stacking the contents to one side. Then, equally carefully, he counted out six packets of banknotes and put them inside one of the boxes.

'Payment,' he said, as much to himself as to Joey.

He stood up. 'I have to get rid of the car.'

Andersen's face looked strange in the torchlight, suspended in the darkness and lit from below so that the eyes seemed deeper. 'I'll leave you the torch. No attempts at escape are necessary. Tomorrow you will be set free: it is all arranged.'

'You think you can fix anything!' Joey tried to sound angry but it didn't convince.

'Yes.'

Joey was left with a couple of sandwiches, a chocolate bar and an apple; and a green bottle of fizzy water with the word 'Perrier' on the label. Joey recognised that: sometimes his mother drank it.

Andersen wasn't gone very long; Joey wondered what he had done with the car.

'In a car park,' said Andersen, 'a rule for agents is always to put things in the obvious place. If you have a secret letter, put it in the mail box.'

'How do you always know what I'm thinking?' said Joey.

Andersen laughed. 'It's your face: a dead giveaway.'

He unrolled the two sleeping bags: one he put in front of the door.

'Bedtime,' he said, 'you can miss cleaning your teeth tonight.'

Joey lay in his sleeping bag watching Andersen as he ate his supper. He ate a lot and quickly; he tipped back a bottle of Perrier.

'Are you very important?'

'I am a Colonel in the KGB,' said Andersen, 'to most Russians that is important.'

He wiped his mouth with the back of his hand, then took off his sweater and unlaced his shoes.

'Sleep,' he said and turned out the torch.

Joey lay awake for a while, thinking over all the things that had happened during the day. Everything was going to plan: Andersen's plan. So much for his hopes of beating him at his own game.

When Joey opened his eyes it was already becoming light.

Andersen, rolled over on his side, was fast asleep, snoring gently.

And sticking out from under his sleeping bag, where he must have put it for safety, was a key. Not *a* key, *the* key . . .

At first it didn't occur to Joey that he might be able to get hold of it. The top half still seemed to be under the bulk of the sleeping Andersen.

But if he could get the key, he could . . .

Andersen's sleeping bag was out of reach. Joey rolled over in that direction and then waited.

Andersen's snoring continued unchecked.

Lying on his stomach Joey stretched out his right arm: he could just reach the key. With great care he pulled gently but firmly: it came free.

Andersen suddenly grunted and stretched out in his sleeping bag; but then relaxed and continued snoring as before.

Joey waited, very still, for a minute, and then picked up the key.

Now what? His heart was beating fast: he could hardly think straight.

Any moment Andersen might wake up.

Get out of the sleeping bag. *Done.* Now put on trainers. *No:* every second counted.

He stood up.

Andersen didn't move.

With just his socks on his feet Joey crossed to the door without a sound. He put the key in the lock.

It couldn't be that simple: it just couldn't.

All he had to do was turn the key in the lock. But it would make a noise, the door would creak as he opened it.

There was nothing for it: NOW!

He unlocked the door and pushed it open. In no time at all he was outside, had pushed the heavy door to and locked it again.

For a couple of seconds he stood listening, shivering with excitement as much as the cold air of the early morning. There wasn't a sound: Andersen had slept through it all.

Joey ran down the service road and onto the main street.
There wasn't anyone in sight.

*

Police Constable Allison had just come on duty. He liked the early morning shift: it meant your afternoons were free.

Boring, though, nothing much ever happened.

Of course, if he could find that American kid and his parents that there was all this fuss about. Every policeman in Britain was on the lookout for them.

What about those two policemen at Heathrow who had let them slip through their fingers? He laughed quietly to himself. They must have had a job explaining that one away . . .

Someone was running towards him, waving his arms: a boy. A boy with no shoes on. At this time of the morning.

Police Constable Allison frowned. 'What's the problem?'

'My name's Joey Medallo,' said the boy, 'and I've captured a Russian spy.'

THIRTEEN

It was ten o'clock before Chalmers arrived. He looked tired and unshaven. He waved to Joey who was sitting in a police van in the service road at the back of the shop units.

He watched while the local Inspector briefed the man from MI6: he could hear every word.

'We were here within twenty minutes of the boy making his escape. I had men posted at the dockside watching the Soviet freighter at about the same time: he definitely hasn't gone on board, in fact nobody has.'

'So he's still inside there.'

'We waited for you to arrive before going in; but he hasn't got past us.'

'There's only one way to find out.'

He held out his hand for the key. The Inspector gave it to him, looking round quickly to check that his men were in position.

'Right!'

Chalmers unlocked the door with one quick movement. He stopped to listen and then pulled the door open.

Joey pressed his nose against the car window.

Chalmers had flattened himself against the wall to one

side of the doorway; everyone was still. Then he stepped forward and vanished into the dark interior.

The policemen outside looked at each other, but nothing happened. There wasn't a sound. What had happened to him?

He reappeared as suddenly as he had vanished, and spread his arms wide.

'He's gone.'

For a moment no one seemed to take it in: and then everyone was talking at once.

Chalmers came across to the car. He was carrying Joey's trainers.

'I expect you could do with these.'

Joey slipped one on to his left foot; but when he tried the other one it stuck. There was something in the toe. He put in his hand and pulled out a piece of screwed-up wrapping paper; he unfolded it and read:

'Dear Joey – This has to be a quick note because I have a lock to pick! What the British Intelligence Service has never done, you almost did – capture *me*! I wish you were on my side! – A.A.'

He handed the note to Chalmers without a word, watching his face as he read it.

'Can I keep it?'

Chalmers nodded and handed it back to him.

Joey refolded the piece of paper and put it in his pocket. Suddenly he was glad that Andersen had got away; but he couldn't have explained why.

'You know, I may even get to like this stuff!' Mrs Medallo put

down her cup of tea and looked at Joey and her husband.

They were in the Central Police Station.

Chalmers, after questioning them closely for five minutes, had vanished with the Station Inspector; a sergeant had brought them tea and biscuits.

Mrs Medallo continued her story: 'So we were in this apartment block with three men guarding us. Then those two other men, the ones we saw at the airport, came yesterday morning and moved us to a farmhouse out in the country. Boy, were they in a hurry! They locked us in the cellar and we could hear them driving away. We thought we were in real trouble, but the police came in the middle of the night and let us out. They had that other man with them.'

'Which other man, mom?'

'You know, the one I said had his hair waved. I just *knew* he was a phoney!'

Dr Medallo nodded. 'Well, they're all in the bag now except this guy Andersen.'

Joey watched his father's face.

'Do you think they'll catch him?'

'It strikes me it's a pretty obvious trail: frankly I wouldn't be surprised if it's a blind.'

It was another half-hour before Chalmers came in to see them. From his set face it was clear that something had gone wrong.

Dr Medallo spoke first: 'He got away.'

'Not on the freighter he didn't. It sailed ten minutes ago but he didn't go on board.'

Joey looked at him. 'But you caught the others.'

'Oh, we caught them all right. I guess we were supposed to – to keep us busy. They know they'll stand trial for Taylor's murder but they aren't saying anything. They're replaceable. It was Andersen that mattered.'

They were silent for a minute, a bit awkward because the British Intelligence man looked so baffled.

At last Dr Medallo stretched out his long legs and put his hands behind his head.

'You know what I think? I think we could do with this guy Andersen on our side.'

Joey turned to his father. 'That's funny. That's just what he said about me!'

FOURTEEN

A small news item in next day's paper told the rest of the story. It was Joey who saw it and read it out to his parents:

'An unidentified motor cruiser, approximately thirty miles south of the Isle of Wight, signalled that it had an injured man on board and was assisted by the Soviet freighter *Lubianka* which was in the vicinity. A coastguard helicopter from Portsmouth, which was quickly on the scene, reported that one person was seen to transfer to the Soviet ship which radioed that no further assistance was required.'

Joey put the paper down: well, that was the end of it.

It was weeks later, back home in the States, that a postcard came for Joey. It was postmarked *Moscow* and had a picture of Red Square on one side.

On the other side was a simple message: 'From Andrei Andersen.'

Joey pinned it up on the wall of his room.